Pedro Maciel

HOW I QUIT BEING GOD

afterword
ANTONIO CICERO

HOW I QUIT BEING GOD
Pedro Maciel

Translated by
Jennifer Sarah Cooper

afterword by
ANTONIO CICERO

EBook Edition

www.zedicoes.com

How I quit being God is an extraordinary story. Pedro Maciel presents us with maxims, epigrams, fragments, reflections, insights of all kinds, from joyous to terrifying, provoking admiration, delight, inspiration and, in some cases even a "hugh?" In short, a free mind exercising its freedom. Always a fascinating spectacle.

Luis Fernando Veríssimo

Absolute knowledge is not within man's reach, and all the bits of knowledge he possesses represent mere crumbs of reality: fragments that, when fortuitous, merely evoke the intangible. However, to reach them, it is necessary to wake from the dream of being God, and embrace the finite and temporal. Perhaps this is why, in some way, time is the true theme of this book, which is a type of **Bildungsroman,** that is to say, an instructive or educative novel. You could say that this intense capacity to ignite the sensibilities, thought and imagination is precisely one of the central charms of *How I Quit Being God.*

Antonio Cícero

How I Quit Being God was, for me, a gratifying surprise, for its originality, for its depth and for the transcendence of the text.

Moacyr Scliar

Man is a god when he dreams, but a beggar when he reflects.
Hölderlin

God is the soul of brutes.
Anonimous

Without God everything is nothing;
and God? Nothing supreme.
E. M. Cioran

Prologue

(...): some civilizations became extinct in the blink of an eye. *We civilizations know now that we are mortal.* **The world is in a state of permanent motion; climatic conditions deteriorate rapidly.** *Man finds nature absurd, or mysterious, or a step-mother. But nature does not exist if not for man. We must act so as not to transgress the universal laws of nature; but, safeguarding these laws, we must conform ourselves to our individual nature.* **Everything is temporary. Don't lend an ear to visionaries. There is no world to discover. The world is already discovered.** (...): this world seems to me not to be my world.

3

Thought is the soul of time. Who do you think you are? *Passing landscapes, basically, nobody.*

7

He thinks he's God, but he doesn´t pass for more than a poor Devil. (...): **the mad house ancestral sorrows.**

8

What keeps us from building bridges over the void? **Metaphysics recalls the world; physics remembers the world at every instant.**

9

- *You shall be as the gods, knowledgeable of good and evil.* **For me, there would only be human gods; the present gods are overly inhumane.**

10

(...) I even hear the murmur of the universe in a passing cloud. *He is a mystic sans God.*

11

'Time' is images of history and landscapes of memory. **Memory will always invent the forgotten.**

13

Thales, the first to inquire about the deities, considered God a spirit that, from the waters, made all things. **Alcmaeon deigned divinity to the sun, moon, stars and the soul.**

14

Pythagoras made God a spirit permeating the nature of all things our souls emanate; **Parmenides, a circle surrounding the sky, sustaining the world with the warmth of light.**

15

(...) light, like the moon, imagines a blue sky.

The Sun's shadow shows over time.

16

Empedocles said gods were the four elements from which all things are made; *Democritus, argues that celestial signs, constellations and their circular motions are gods, argues that nature projects these images and later our science and understanding of them.*

17

Plato proclaimed his beliefs in various ways: in the 'Timeaus', he says, the father of the world cannot be designed; in 'The laws', we should not ask about his being; and at other moments, in these same books, gods are said to be the world, the sky, the stars, the Earth and our very souls; **Thank God, nobody is God!**

18

Myths understood me; do you understand me? **The Devil is a version of God; God is a verse by the Devil.**

19

Speusippus, Plato's nephew, said that God is a particular force that governs everything and is animate; *Strato of Lampsacus, that it is nature with the power to generate, increase or decrease, shapeless and unfeeling.*

20

Xenocrates says there are eight gods: the five named among the planets, the sixth comprising all the fixed stars as their members, the seventh and eighth the Sun and the moon. **Diogenes of Apollonia says that God is time.**

21

(...): I can't be bothered with lost things, just lost time. **The wind never returned my time.**

22

Aristo considered the form of God incomprehensible, senseless, and disregards the issue of whether inanimate or something else; *for Cleanthes, now reason, now the world, now the spirit of nature, now the supreme heat that surrounds and envelops the world.*

23

Persaeus, disciple of Zeno, held that surnamed were the gods who brought any notable benefit to humankind. **God is the only being that, to reign, doesn't even need to exit.**

24

(...); gods are Godless when remembering man. **Forgetfulness is an allegory of the memory.**

25

Chryssipus made a confusing overview of all former opinions and included, among the thousand forms of gods he contemplates, man who is also immortalized. **(...) there is a terrifying power in those who venerate the gods.**

26

When gods no longer existed, and Christ was yet to exist, there was, from Cicero to Marcus Aurelius a singular moment when only man existed, **(...): from the bottom of his heart, man aspires to recapture the condition before acquiring consciousness. History is merely the detour he took to get there.**

27

My younger brother killed himself to become God. *(...) for now this is still the time of tragedy, the time of morals and religions.*

28

: for the love of God go to Hell. God
is a *good Devil.*

29

*As for me, I always thought gods existed, and
I have always proclaimed this; but I don't believe they care what humans do.* **To live in
suspended time, as a god.**

30

**(...); for 'centuries' nobody an-
nounces the end of the world.** *I am
my world.*

31

(...): of the divinities to whom were given a body, so that people could have a religion, within this universal blindness, it seems to me I would have more easily sided with the Sun worshippers. **One day, beyond space and time, I'll find out where it is still, why it is then and if there is sun.**

32

I am the Alpha and the Omega, the beginning and the end, says the Lord God: that which is, was, and ever shall be, the Almighty. **If God existed everyone would surely find out.**

33

Forgetting as a pastime. **The eyes of memory, with time, begin wearing glasses.**

34

Mystics 'think' reality is beyond thought. **I think extensively on this thought (…).**

35

The spirit remains in time and not in space. *I have never had any other prison aside from my body.*

36

(…) utopia: *seek first the kingdom of God, and all shall be granted you.* **For one day, I believed everything could be done.**

37

Thought is always beyond the body.
Language is the mask of thought.

38

(...); comets are born with their goals already mapped. *There is nothing more treacherous than superstition, which covers its crimes with the will of the gods.*

39

'I' died in 2046. *There is no alliance so great between heaven and us that with our death the light of the stars should die as well.*

40

(...): he noted attentively each ray of lightning that plunged into the lake- he insisted on measuring the length of the rays to unveil how many mirrors could clarify the night. **His hour is not this time. Yesterday he got lost in the past and raced to get ahead, but didn't stop further on as if it were before.** He continued foraging, forging ahead, living and dying every day. Every day is a memory.

41

The dream, this flight from solitude.
Often times, I no longer differentiate my thoughts before sleep. I don't even know if I've slept.

43

(...): there may be no dreams, but there are many realities to be realized. **The nightmare is an oracle.**

44

(...); I woke to the incessant murmur, a voice I hadn't heard in ages, noises of invisible winds; almost inaudible whisper. **We inherit from our ancestors, emotions not notions.**

45

He does not know who he was, who he is and who he shall be. *Sometimes he looks at himself as if he were some other despite being the same as ever.*

46

I never obsess over the abyss. **The other day I faced the Sun for a long time; was almost blinded.**

47

Sometimes I feel like Dante returning from Hell. There are heads that, even cut off, emit thoughts.

48

He put an end to his own life as a question of principle. *If, at the hour of his death, all of the compassion of others banded together to stop him from leaving, this man would not die,*

49

(...): to survive beyond my time. **Time is no longer for me so far from every-thing.**

50

I am not of this world.(...): *to belong in the world one need get along with the world.*

51

(...): he spends hours under the shadow of a tree noticing his own shadow. **My shadow never wears a mask.**

52

He arrived yesterday, but already took everyone's time, as always. **Nowadays go late.**

54

Don't waste your time with jackasses! **The times are remote; only life is recent.**

55

— The day-in-day-out (time) is the history of the memory. I don't know if I should turn or return.

56

Silence, time's inner space. *I know I have the best time and space —and that I was never measured, nor could I ever be.*

57

(...): I should be cremated and the ashes thrown to the wind. Don't bury me in some weed ridden garden and eras already rid of memory; *undesired remembrances come to me and not the forgetting I desire.*

62

Almost everyone speaks of themselves as if they were the best of human beings. *Nothing is as difficult as not fooling yourself.*

63

I look at the heavens as if they were hiding one of the doors to Hell. **The blind topple the stars.**

65

(...); from what have I most suffered? *Perhaps the habit of developing my entire thought — to reach the end of my very self.*

66

(...); some, under the yellow moon, grow green-eyed over others. **Cultivate an enemy to one day forgive him.**

67

(...) there is no argument that doesn't have its contrary. **Contradiction moves the world – all things contradict themselves.**

68

(...): one day he is going to attack time. **Time is a fable.**

69

I go around losing time, like Marcel Proust. *Time passes the moment something is far away from me.*

70

(...) in the beginning, the gods created the heavens and the Earth. *I tried to write Paradise, they don't move, hear the wind speak, this is Paradise (…).*

72

The diary, the time where you hide from life. *Time flies in the middle of the night.*

73

(...); I even try to hear the explosion that would have originated the cos-mos. *For the love of God free me from God.*

74

: these days the Sun rolls alone with its head in the clouds. I look up to clouds that come from so far and have no idea where they are going to.

75

Landscape - (illusion of the scape). An infinity in each glimpse.

76

(...): astrophysics, mathematics and music cannot free themselves from their exact abstractions. It´s *normal for me to feel strange.*

77

Lyrical: logic has its magic. *It has already been said that God can create everything, except for anything that is contrary to the laws of logic. — It's just that we would not be capable of saying what an "illogical" world would be like.*

78

Sometimes the world is abysmal. (...); *I saw you where I am not unless heaven or earth.*

79

(...): *before, they knew nothing of the glory of thinking of others, living for others, which is now so commonplace.* **I know of no humanist who is a moralist.**

80

(...), *an average man rarely concerns himself about other living beings with the same intensity and persistence that he exhibits toward his car.* **The moralist is immoral.**

81

(...); *according to our moral fashion, they would have to be called immoral, since they fought with all the force of their egos and against empathy for others (above all thesuffering and weak).* **The moral; pure psychology.**

82

Nobody likes to get a moral lesson; I like to get coca-cola. (...) I´ve done only what I feel like doing; life seems perfect to me.

83

The vices of yesterday have become the customs of today. **Why go back to being one's self again?**

84

Moralists have short memories. *From the moral point of view, we still live in a neolithic era, or rather, we are not altogether rudimentary, and, however, we haven't yet moved out of the greatest rudimentary stage or one that can justify any celebration.*

85

Orlando spent hours and hours observing the circles under Virginia's eyes. *The ogling of time.*

86

I live blindly. **My shadow looks for me.**

87

(...); those closest take us far from ourselves. We no longer forget fleeting things, after remembering them.

88

My friend Virgil drowned trying to save Ulysses and Penelope. The sea was not fit for fishing.

89

Could the sea winds be the thoughts of gods? *When I die I'll return to search for the moments I didn't live by the sea.*

90

(...); I took the day today to experience instantaneous sensations: sensations that are the perception of a time when the world began, and from whence, almost everything is successive. *Gods, do not judge me as a god, but as a man destroyed by the sea.*

91

There are days that last longer in others. Existence as a pastime?

92

– It's always good to keep a certain distance from those closest. *After certain fits of eternity and fever, we ask ourselves why reason does not deign us to be gods.*

93

Present time escapes us. Stopped hours; wind in the leaves.

95

April twilights do not have their own light. *I know well the light of my abysses.*

96

Why not doubt in lightning? Leave tomorrow for tomorrow!

97

Pair up with a cloud out of air. **The sky pretends it sleeps.**

100

He is 'awed' like any other 'god'. I'm
inconsolable in my solitude; I no longer
feel such solace.

101

(...); what have I lost if not time? *No-*
body has lived in the past, nobody will live in
the future; the present is the form of all life.

102

What is not thought is also thought.
We never think that what we think hides from
us what we are.

115

(...): he watched attentively each ray of lightning that plunged into the lake; insisted on measuring the length of the rays to unveil how many mirrors light up a night.

116

His hour is not this time. Yesterday he got lost in the past and raced to get ahead, but didn't stop further on as if it were sometime before.

117

(...) he went on rambling, scrambling, living and dying each day. **Every day is a memory.**

119

Idiots never lie. A man is always victim of his own truths.

120

Thought invents language; remem-brance reinvents the landscape; *Life is the real philosophy and philosophy is ideal life.*

121

Yesterday I visited my hometown; nobody recognized me. *God is not revealed 'in' the world.*

139

I never sought a place to have gone to. I ask in vain where to go. **Only time goes!**

143

(...): the mad could never circulate freely around the heart or the outskirts of my city. Many died feigning lucidity.

146

What makes me laugh is not our madness; it's our knowledge. **What does time want? To sigh. What does the temple want? To hide.**

151

Remembrances learn to take their leave. **Every forgetting is the faking of thinking.**

158

(...): so often my words were not to be spoken; so often truth is in keeping quiet. **Silence deafens the despair.**

159

(...); still before sunrise when I heard the first fruits ripening the day. My shadow does not like to sunbathe.

166

Late: finite falls at the right time. *I need time in order to be brief.*

167

I go on improvising remembrances. **There are moments when I think without thoughts.**

168

Reality, this recent time; **metaphor of existence.**

178

Memory is the delusion of the mad.
Remembrances speak for me; I listen to
all in silence.

180

**Where can I be just an abstract
being?** When does the word recover its
precise sense?

187

(...); the awareness of feeling happy.
*Why is it that, to be happy, it's necessary not
to know it?*

193

Unlearn: teach yourself. *Whoever believes that we can know nothing doesn't know at all if we know enough to affirm we know nothing.*

197

The dream, this time in which I am nobody.**(...); now I'll concentrate on opening my eyes without disrupting the landscape.**

256

All existence is a legend of time. *Between the phantasm and myself, it seems to me that one of us must disappear...*

333

(...): God, inspiration of the crazed.
Reading poems aloud irritates the retired gods.

488

Look! **I have all the dreams in the world; I just don't know how to make them come true.**

500

Look at landscape: 'time' is nobody's bitch. **What is there in this sunny shadow if not me myself?**

525

**Yesterday I decided not to exist in-
side myself.** That didn't last very long.

545

All history is a daily conversation. **The
past like a promise.**

547

*A man without hope and who is aware of
being so no longer belongs to the future.* **He
made of his hopelessness a lesson.**

552

Cloudless day, clear, blue; it's the passage of time. We look at each other eye to eye (…).

566

Darkness, this emptiness of time. *To die, to sleep, perhaps to dream.*

595

(…), the journal says almost everything; life as the only exit. *I want to live in the participle imperative of the future, in the passive voice — in the "must be".*

650

(...), feeling is always some thinking that didn't have time to express it-self in any other way. *Expression begins when the thought ends.*

677

(...); thinking is relearning how to see, direct one's own awareness, make of each image a privileged place. **At times I imagine re-membrances without images.**

705

Memory, a river that drains and disap-pears. **Lost time; life updated.**

753

(...); *what are these churches still, if not mausoleums and tombs of God?* **I am God of myself.**

770

God can do nothing without us. **God's dream is to live my life.**

807

Sociology: to bear a life of forgetting. There are certain days I bear away from my own self.

828

It's necessary to have faith in the hopelessness. I don't expect anything from the gods; nor do they expect anything from me.

900

(...): I still haven't seen any image that isn't the memory of a landscape. *I am the awareness of the landscape.*

913

Whoever picks a flower pisses off a star. **(...); the delicacy of the spirit of a pig.**

921

(...): *words go where thoughts go;* thoughts unravel thinking, ramble incessantly, without knowing why, whether solitude or passion. Could it be that this thought has something to do with what I'm thinking? **Language always hides thought. Thinking twice, we need to stop and think.** No one can save us from our thoughts.

929

(...): when I find myself alone, I fill the emptiness left by others. Silencing to disenchant.

931

Each night is an east. Day, like an eternity.

937

I don't think of returning to the 'beyond' to relive what already 'was'. **Eternity already is.**

977

My God, why have you forsaken me? **(...) at the bottom of the lake, a shipwreck.**

999

(...): time always goes slower than thought. **We think we are eternal.**

1020

Time is landscape, because it is spacing. (...); sometimes I don't know if time is imagined by me or if it is lived in me.

1144

Hope: the anthropology of feeling, a thought of the desperate. **You could say that your hope is the disaster of your destiny.**

1146

He invents other names for things; calls morning stone, twilight and night penumbra. *Not on time, if not in time, God created the heavens and earth.*

1148

: the soul needs to torture itself to manifest. *Gods should not remain homeless, and souls without spectacles.*

1159

People call on God to obtain the impossible.
For the possible, man suffices.

1163

There is too much optimism in the ignorant! *What man has the most difficulty understanding, from time immemorial until now, is his own ignorance about himself!*

1164

Thinkers routinely complain of headaches. To dream, and, afterward, to remember: therein lies the thought.

1200

Could you return my revolution? **We are exiled from our own time, according to the theory of relativity.**

1210

All remembrances unremember themselves in other remembrances. **Memorable lapses of memory.**

1220

Disillusions: some illusions are already born without luminescence. **Shadows should only accompany us in the off hours.**

1225

Why all the effort to be like them? **One day I will be the other me.**

1227

: meantime begets more time. The times as sentence.

1229

(...); vile and abject thing is man, if he does not raise himself above humanity. **The suffering of poets, artists and saints take on the spiritual dung of humanity.**

1230

(...): end of the world: rumination of the mornings. Resurrection of the dead. Lamentations. Rivers of tears. Human sacrifices. Exercises in style. Games of chance. Ponderings of Phaedrus. Mythological evocations. The logic of science. The uselessness of astrology. **Awareness of all. Continuum of time; history. All the time; existence. The final hour. The infinite hour. All the time in the world.**

1259

Destiny does not always make sense.
A man's character is his destiny.

1265

Each time is a story. **Every end is an immensity.**

1270

(...): the Sun goes dries out the soil soaked with my shadows. The shadow, illusion of time.

1300

(...); today I was thinking out loud when a clumsy bee fell in my soup. *Man thinks and God laughs.*

1303

: to unshadow solitude over time. **The infinite, this perfect time of solitude.**

1313

When I was born, the gods were already dead. *If I could, I would dedicate this book to God.*

1321

How many of my readers perceive that these writings can be understood however they wish? *My ambition is to say in ten phrases what anyone else says in a book — what anyone else 'doesn't' say in a book.*

1322

(...): there is writing that is so sonorous it can be read with eyes closed. *The true reader has to be the author amplified.*

1325

(...), I don't write about my life because I believe that I live another life when I write. *When stories are told adequately there is no more need for novels.*

1333

Do I find myself because I no longer look for you? *In the winter a Buddhist in the summer a nudist.*

1337

There are spirits that live suspended in time. **Dispirited; tread lightly on the spirits.**

1339

Meanwhile: I always think about that space of time between being and not being. **He seems to be from another world that is not our own.**

1340

(...): *words go where thoughts go;* **Thoughts scramble thinking, ramble almost incessantly, no one knows why, whether it's solitude, whether it's passion.**

1344

Could this thought have something to do with what I am thinking? **Language always hides thought.**

1353

Thinking twice, we need to stop and think. **No one can save us from our own thoughts.**

1363

I'm just one step away from becoming human. For a long time, I felt like any old god.

1365

A god for each dead. *I was born 'many' and I died 'one' alone.*

1366

Why does one live an entire life without knowing why? *Time goes by, and the years arrive...*

1500

I find myself close to my longings. **(...)
poets hover over abysses.**

1600

**Everything is philosophy, but not
everything is poetry.** *Philosophy could be
much more expressive like poetry.*

1700

How much time is lost collecting recol-
lections? **There are days that are like
poems, useless.**

1730

(…); of the spirit's operations, the least frequent is reason. **He wandered from morning to night trying to give meaning to the nothing.**

1733

Madness is a mask; *don't blame the mirror for your twisted face.*

1821

He only recovered his mental health after giving his goodbyes to the gods. **Thought is the world's sentiment, not time's.**

1907

Everything in life is by approximation: from mathematics to love. *Time I leave to the wind.*

1908

Meditate; edit me. He never says what he feels or thinks.

1909

What do they know of me? *Each one forges a god for himself.*

1959

The world is not always reborn when we rise on the morrow. **(...): tomorrow I'm going to presence my absence.**

1968

(...): the end of time announces other ends. *My end is in my beginning and my beginning is in my end.*

1979

(...): end of the world: morning ruminations. Resurrection of the dead.

2000

(...): lamentations. River of tears. Human Sacrifice. **Exercises in style. Games of chance.**

2009

Ponderings of Phaedrus. Mythological reminiscence. **The logic of Science. The futility of astrology.**

2027

Aware of everything. Time Continuum; history. All the time; existence. The final hour. The infinite hour. All the time in the world.

2033

The Sun has a shadow so bright that you can see the light of night. Some civilizations became extinct in the blink of an eye.

2041

Don't lend an ear to visionaries. (...) **there is no world to discover.**

2046

The world is already discovered; this world seems to me not to be my world.

To all and to none

Afterword

How I quit being God resembles the title of a book of memoirs or a novel. On opening it and leafing through it, however, the first impression you get is a book of aphorisms. Nonetheless, while an aphorism is something complete in and of itself, many of the syntagms that comprise *How I quit being God* are fragments. Take, for example, syntagm n° 7, "He thinks he's a God, but doesn't pass for more than a poor Devil. (...): **the mad house ancestral sorrows**". The ellipses in the parentheses indicate that this is a fragment. Within this very fragment, the use of bold after the colon establishes an enigmatic distinction between the two components: perhaps the sentence highlighted is hierarchically superior to the other; perhaps it consists of a quote; or perhaps it's none of that, and there is some other explanation for the emphasis, that we have yet to rationalize. In any case, the artifice accentuates the fragmentary character of the syntagm in question.

Something analogous should be observed with respect to the book as a whole. There is, naturally, something open in the entire book of aphorisms. One can suppose that it would be possible to suppress and/or add specific aphorisms to such a book, without sacrificing its tone, that is, the specific unit of its totality. Nonetheless, for this same reason, one normally cannot say that a book of aphorisms does not constitute, in its own way, a totality. Now, also on this point, *How I quit being God*, differs from other traditional books of aphorisms. The prologue itself is fragmentary. Besides this, the book begins with aphorism n° 3, and then jumps to number 7, continuing in the natural order of succession up to n° 41, then jumps to n° 43, etc. In any case, according to my calculations, the book contains nearly four hundred aphorisms, and the last being number 2046. *How I quit being God* is presented, however, as if it consisted of a selection of fragments – and, many times, as we have seen, fragments of fragments – of a book or notebook to which we do not have access. Here we play on the difference between aphorism and fragment: neither the aphorism nor the book of

aphorisms necessarily point to some other
totality, besides that which they themselves
constitute; while the fragment points to a
totality – even if lost, or yet to be con-
quered, or fictitious, or all of these – ab-
sent, and from which it is a fragment.
The missing totality can be a book of
aphorisms; but it can also be a notebook of
notations or a journal or a book of memoirs; and it can be conceived as having been
written by the very same author or a character of his: it can, in other words be factu-
al or fictional. Is it important for the reader
to choose between one of these possibili-
ties to the exclusion of the others? No. The
important thing is that all of them are presented to the reader. This is revealed in the
clarifying confusion of fragment n° 929:
"(...), I don't write about my life because I
believe that I live another life when I
write."
Besides this, just as the aphorisms, these
fragments of aphorisms, being, simultane-
ously, thought and image, understanding
and feeling, particularity and universality,
escape all genres. In this way, we return to
the first impression that we mentioned,
that is, that *How I quit being God* constitutes

a book of memoirs or a novel. As it guides us by the title, it is a book that describes the process (real or fictional) through which the narrator (real or fictional) quits (literally or metaphorically) being God. Fragment nº 1363 seems to confirm this thesis. It states: "I am one step away from becoming human. For the longest time, I felt as if I were any old god." Along this line, *How I quit being God* can be taken as a kind of *Bildungsroman,* that is, an informative or formative novel, fragmentarily relating the process – it being fragmentary itself – through which one becomes or accepts oneself as a human being.

If we embark on this interpretation, the epigram by Holderlin – "Man is a god when he dreams, but a beggar when he reflects"—, whose first meaning, for the German poet, was of exalting the imagination, in comparison with the understanding, must, re-contextualized, acquire another meaning. In this case, if man is a god when he dreams, it is because he dreams of being God. On waking and reflecting, however, he recognizes himself and his finiteness and temporality, in opposition to the infinite and eternity of which he dreams. As fragment n° 1733 states, "He only recovered his mental health after giving the goodbye to the gods." Also, omniscience was a dream. Absolute knowledge is not within man's reach, and everything he knows is just begged-for crumbs of reality: fragments that, when fortuitous, merely evoke the intangible. However, to reach them, it is necessary to wake from the dream of being God and embrace the finite and temporal. Could it be perhaps that, in some way, time is the true theme of this book.

But just so the reader is not fooled: spurred by some of his thoughts, I could not resist the temptation here to express, however schematically, my own interpretation of a specific aspect of *How I quit being God.* It amounts to just one of innumerable possible interpretations. In fragment n° 1321, the author asks himself: "How many of my readers perceive that these writings can be understood any way they wish?" My answer: the true readers. Each will, no doubt, question for him or herself each fragment: questioning whether it is true or not; in what measure; how it dialogues with the others; to what other texts it alludes; what

consequences arise from them; etc. And
they will do the same with the book as a
whole. And it is precisely this intense capacity to ignite the sensibilities, thought
and imagination that constitutes one of the
central charms of *How I quit being God.*

Antonio Cicero

PEDRO MACIEL, according to poet and translator, Ivo Barroso, "makes us believe that Brazilian literature can still produce something new, but that curiously dates back to the very art of writing: style. His first novel, The Hour of the Shipwrecked - *A Hora dos Náufragos* (Bertrand Brasil, 2006), disturbs through the force of its language. The closest thing there is to this book is Bauldelaire's famous *fussées*".

www.ingramcontent.com/pod-product-compliance
Lightning Source LLC
Chambersburg PA
CBHW061538120726
48001CB00004B/1618